Belongs To

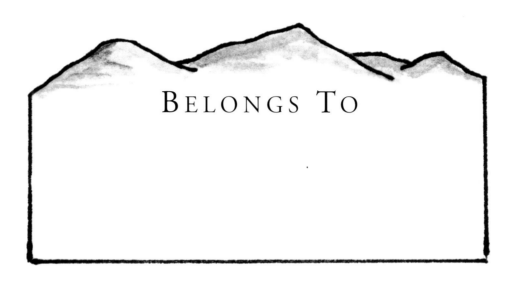

Always Treat others -
people & animals -
with Kindness & respect!
Cowgirl Pey

Jazmine

DEDICATION

With Love To

my two "grown" children: Kimberley and Sean.

Watching them "spread their wings

and learn to fly" truly enriched my life.

They continue to be not only my "children"

but also two very special friends.

Also a big "thank you"

to Dr. Bruce and Kris Bordelon

of the K-M Regional Animal Hospital, Kasson, MN:

two very special friends

who do wonders for animals in need.

LIBRARY OF CONGRESS CATALOGING-IN-PUBLICATION DATA
Sundberg, Peggy.
Jazmine's Incredible Story, The True Adventures of Cowgirl Peg's Beloved Companion
p. cm.
ISBN 0-9721057-5-1 HARDCOVER
1. Title — Author — Cowgirl Peg. 2. Juv. Lit.
3. Dogs — pets — animal rescue — animal abuse
— animal shelters — character traits.
2005910156

Second edition printed in Canada by Friesens

PUBLISHED BY: Cowgirl Peg Enterprises
P.O. Box 56, Wheatland, WY 82201
cowgirlpeg2@gmail.com
www.cowgirlpeg.com

COPYRIGHT: 2006 © Peggy Sundberg
DESIGN BY: F + P Graphic Design, Inc., Fort Collins, CO
COVER PHOTOGRAPHY: Jon Sheppard Photography, Avon, CO

Jazmine's
Incredible Story

The True Adventures of Cowgirl Peg's Beloved Companion

Peggy Sundberg

Watercolors by
Pat Wiles

Believe it or not,
everything in this book really happened!

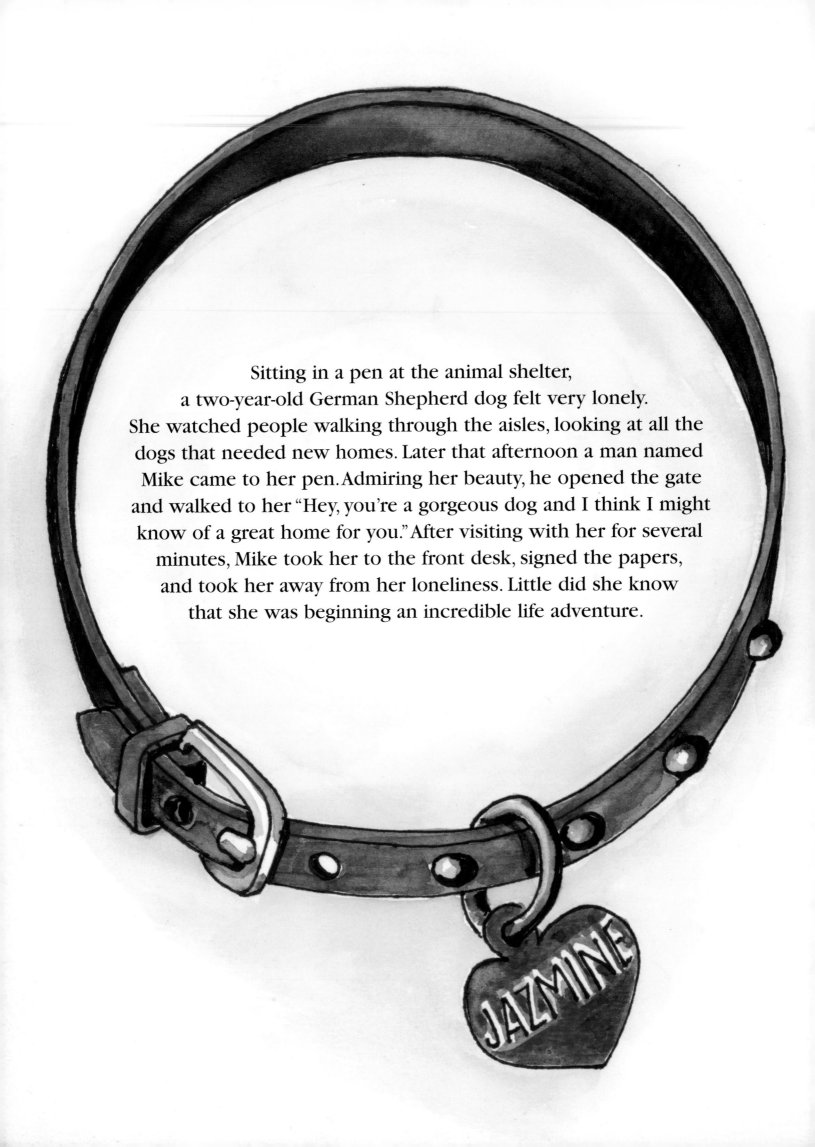

Sitting in a pen at the animal shelter,
a two-year-old German Shepherd dog felt very lonely.
She watched people walking through the aisles, looking at all the
dogs that needed new homes. Later that afternoon a man named
Mike came to her pen. Admiring her beauty, he opened the gate
and walked to her "Hey, you're a gorgeous dog and I think I might
know of a great home for you." After visiting with her for several
minutes, Mike took her to the front desk, signed the papers,
and took her away from her loneliness. Little did she know
that she was beginning an incredible life adventure.

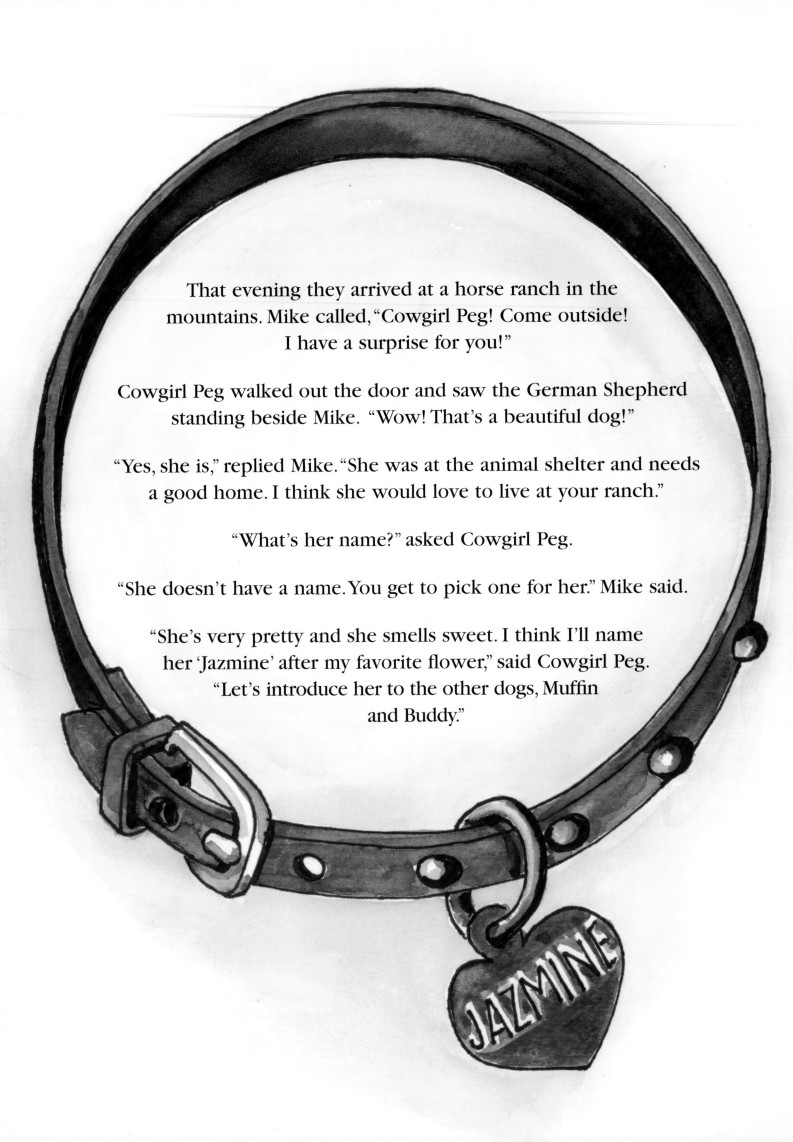

That evening they arrived at a horse ranch in the mountains. Mike called, "Cowgirl Peg! Come outside! I have a surprise for you!"

Cowgirl Peg walked out the door and saw the German Shepherd standing beside Mike. "Wow! That's a beautiful dog!"

"Yes, she is," replied Mike. "She was at the animal shelter and needs a good home. I think she would love to live at your ranch."

"What's her name?" asked Cowgirl Peg.

"She doesn't have a name. You get to pick one for her." Mike said.

"She's very pretty and she smells sweet. I think I'll name her 'Jazmine' after my favorite flower," said Cowgirl Peg. "Let's introduce her to the other dogs, Muffin and Buddy."

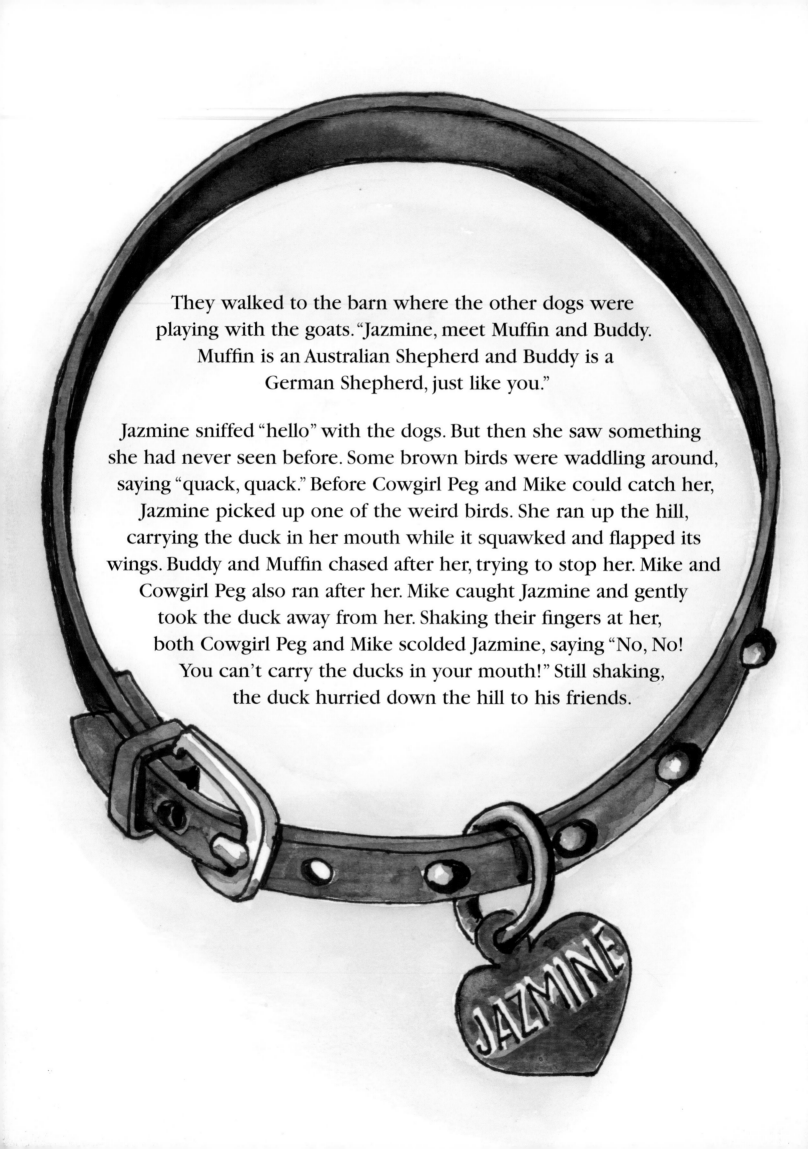

They walked to the barn where the other dogs were playing with the goats. "Jazmine, meet Muffin and Buddy. Muffin is an Australian Shepherd and Buddy is a German Shepherd, just like you."

Jazmine sniffed "hello" with the dogs. But then she saw something she had never seen before. Some brown birds were waddling around, saying "quack, quack." Before Cowgirl Peg and Mike could catch her, Jazmine picked up one of the weird birds. She ran up the hill, carrying the duck in her mouth while it squawked and flapped its wings. Buddy and Muffin chased after her, trying to stop her. Mike and Cowgirl Peg also ran after her. Mike caught Jazmine and gently took the duck away from her. Shaking their fingers at her, both Cowgirl Peg and Mike scolded Jazmine, saying "No, No! You can't carry the ducks in your mouth!" Still shaking, the duck hurried down the hill to his friends.

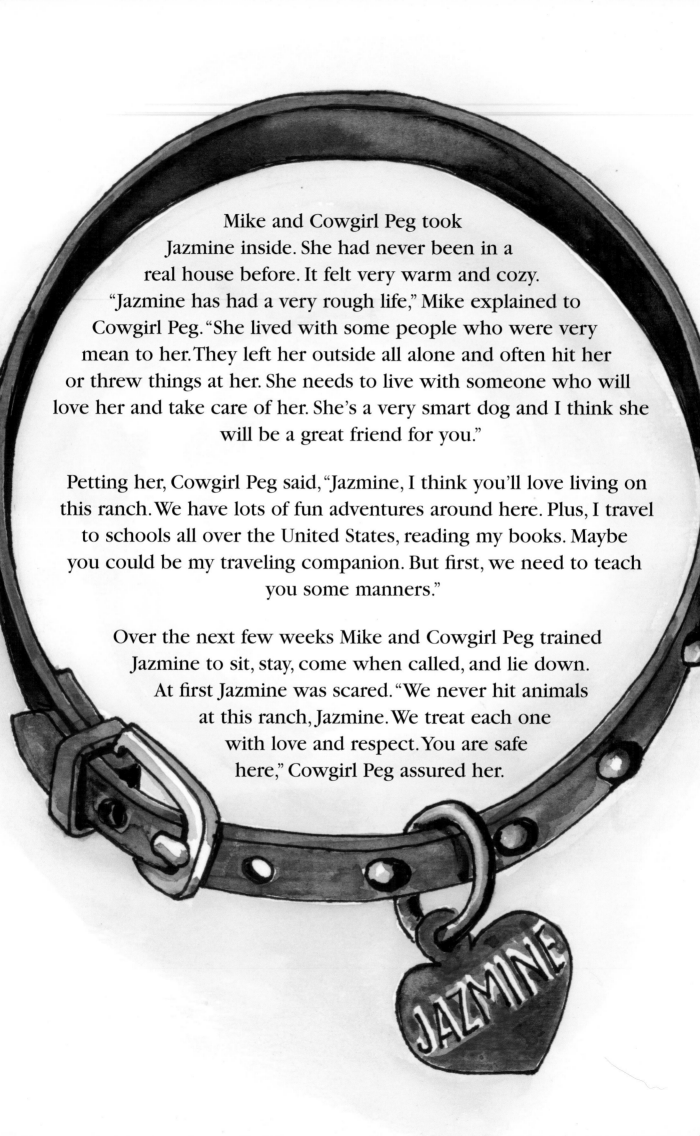

Mike and Cowgirl Peg took
Jazmine inside. She had never been in a
real house before. It felt very warm and cozy.
"Jazmine has had a very rough life," Mike explained to
Cowgirl Peg. "She lived with some people who were very
mean to her. They left her outside all alone and often hit her
or threw things at her. She needs to live with someone who will
love her and take care of her. She's a very smart dog and I think she
will be a great friend for you."

Petting her, Cowgirl Peg said, "Jazmine, I think you'll love living on
this ranch. We have lots of fun adventures around here. Plus, I travel
to schools all over the United States, reading my books. Maybe
you could be my traveling companion. But first, we need to teach
you some manners."

Over the next few weeks Mike and Cowgirl Peg trained
Jazmine to sit, stay, come when called, and lie down.
At first Jazmine was scared. "We never hit animals
at this ranch, Jazmine. We treat each one
with love and respect. You are safe
here," Cowgirl Peg assured her.

JAZMINE

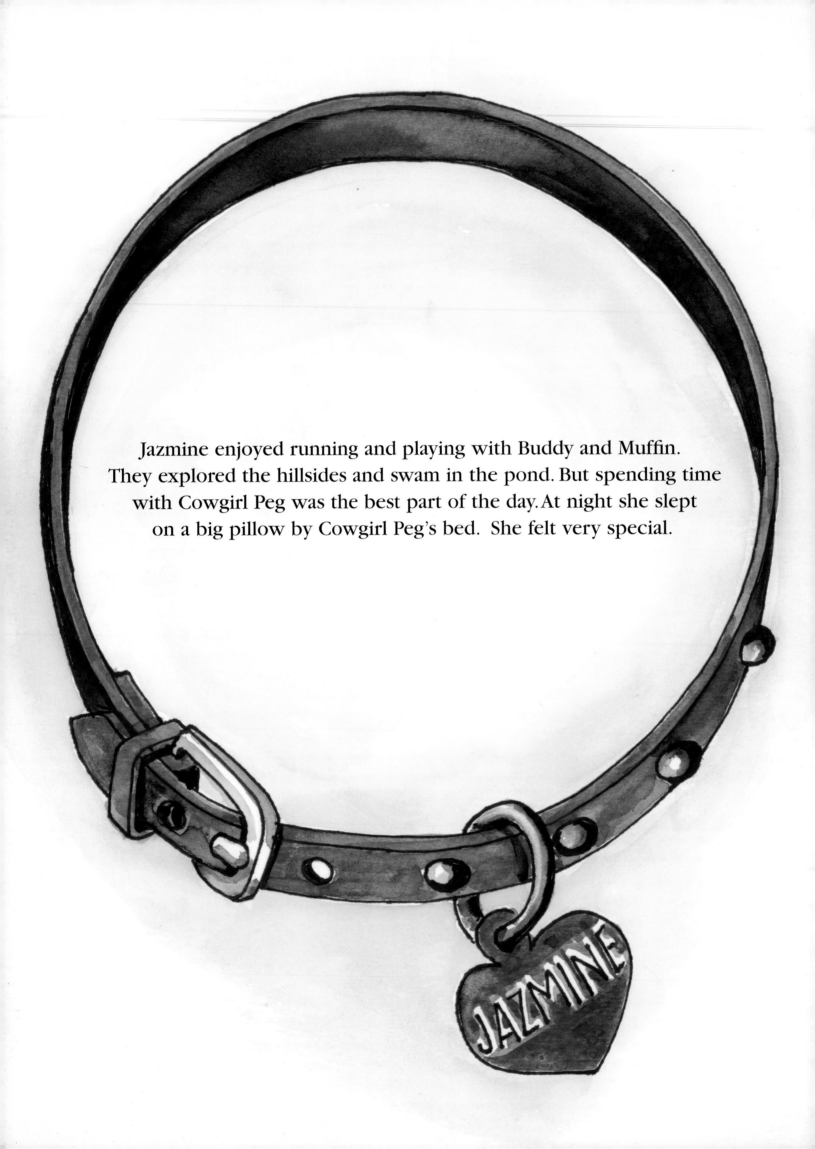

Jazmine enjoyed running and playing with Buddy and Muffin.
They explored the hillsides and swam in the pond. But spending time
with Cowgirl Peg was the best part of the day. At night she slept
on a big pillow by Cowgirl Peg's bed. She felt very special.

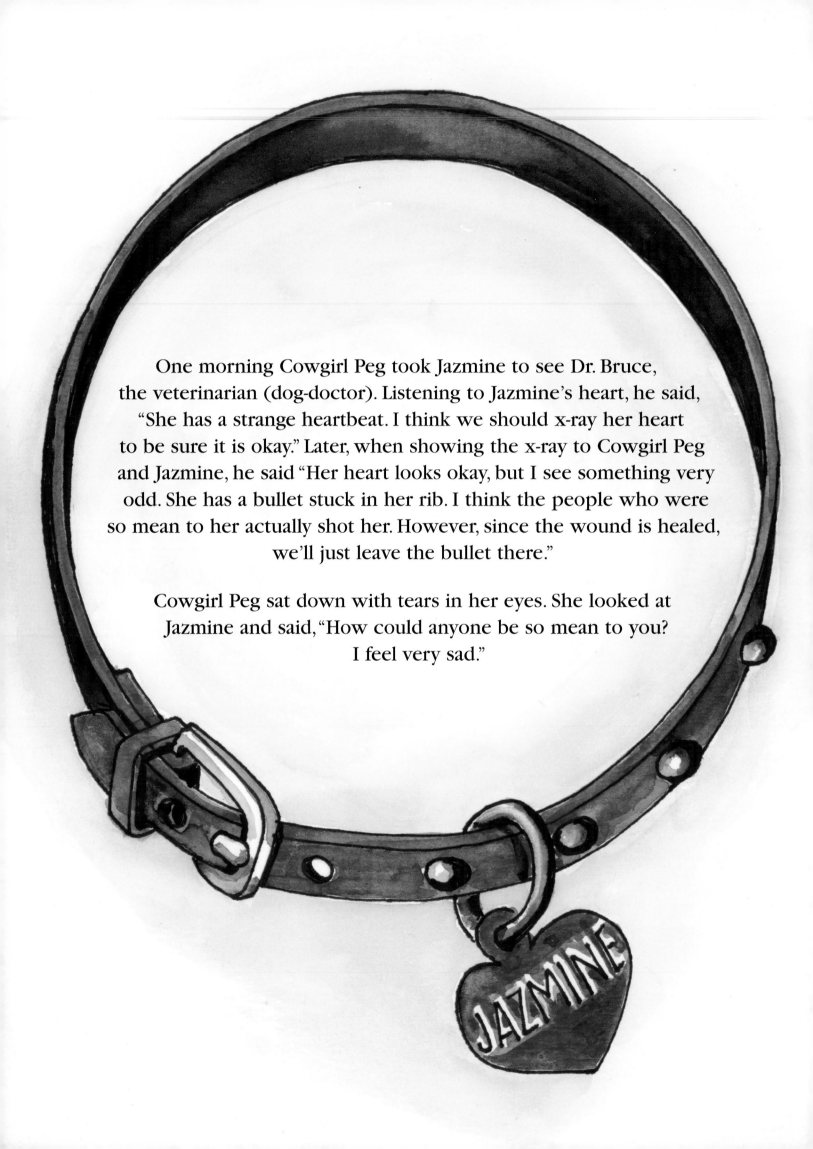

One morning Cowgirl Peg took Jazmine to see Dr. Bruce,
the veterinarian (dog-doctor). Listening to Jazmine's heart, he said,
"She has a strange heartbeat. I think we should x-ray her heart
to be sure it is okay." Later, when showing the x-ray to Cowgirl Peg
and Jazmine, he said "Her heart looks okay, but I see something very
odd. She has a bullet stuck in her rib. I think the people who were
so mean to her actually shot her. However, since the wound is healed,
we'll just leave the bullet there."

Cowgirl Peg sat down with tears in her eyes. She looked at
Jazmine and said, "How could anyone be so mean to you?
I feel very sad."

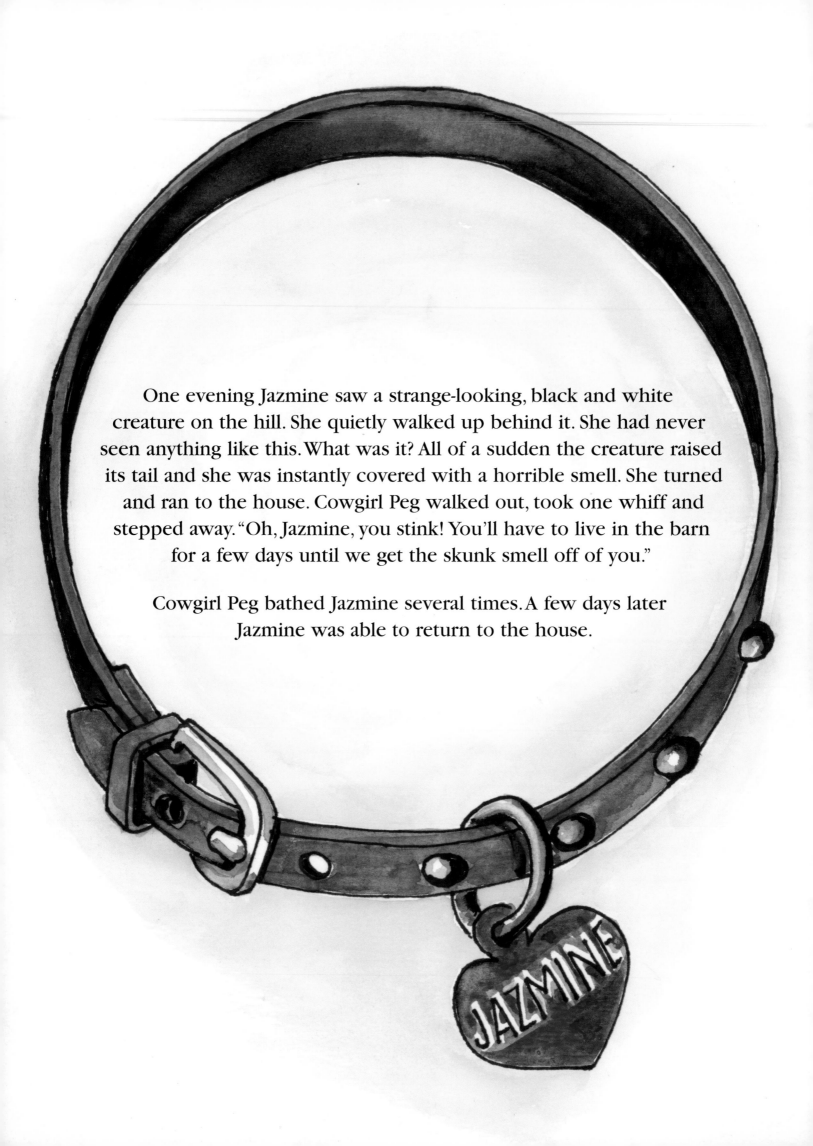

One evening Jazmine saw a strange-looking, black and white creature on the hill. She quietly walked up behind it. She had never seen anything like this. What was it? All of a sudden the creature raised its tail and she was instantly covered with a horrible smell. She turned and ran to the house. Cowgirl Peg walked out, took one whiff and stepped away. "Oh, Jazmine, you stink! You'll have to live in the barn for a few days until we get the skunk smell off of you."

Cowgirl Peg bathed Jazmine several times. A few days later Jazmine was able to return to the house.

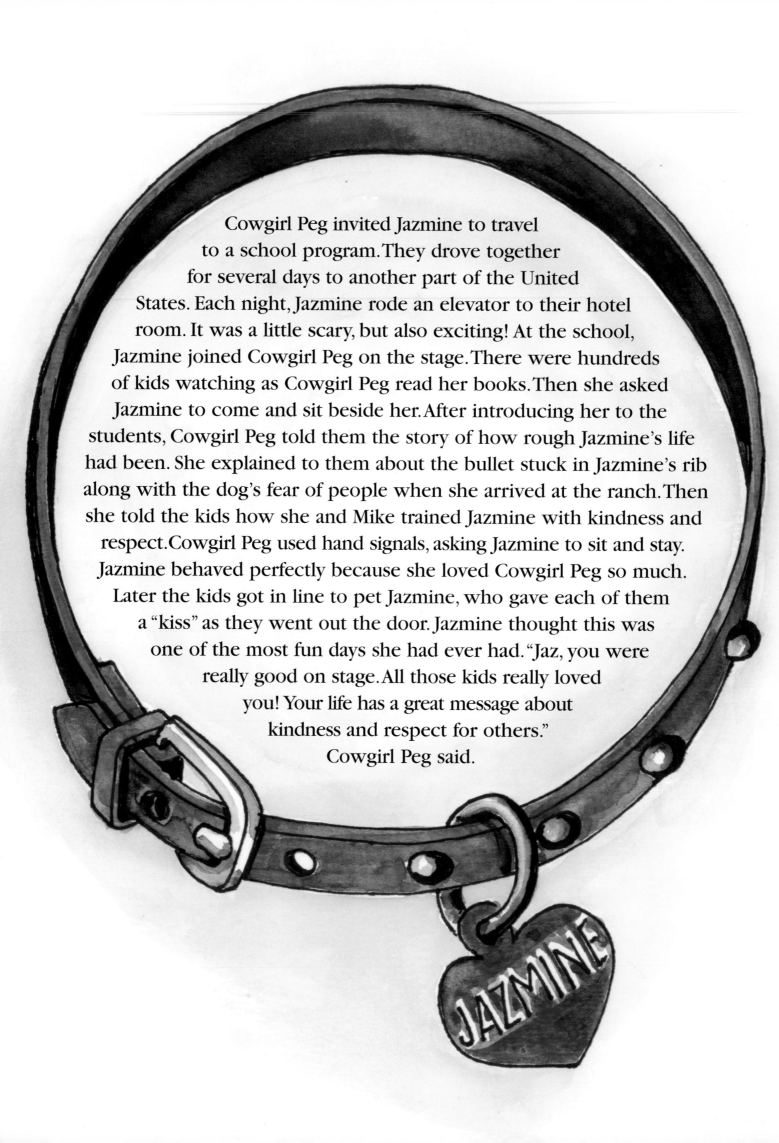

Cowgirl Peg invited Jazmine to travel
to a school program. They drove together
for several days to another part of the United
States. Each night, Jazmine rode an elevator to their hotel
room. It was a little scary, but also exciting! At the school,
Jazmine joined Cowgirl Peg on the stage. There were hundreds
of kids watching as Cowgirl Peg read her books. Then she asked
Jazmine to come and sit beside her. After introducing her to the
students, Cowgirl Peg told them the story of how rough Jazmine's life
had been. She explained to them about the bullet stuck in Jazmine's rib
along with the dog's fear of people when she arrived at the ranch. Then
she told the kids how she and Mike trained Jazmine with kindness and
respect. Cowgirl Peg used hand signals, asking Jazmine to sit and stay.
Jazmine behaved perfectly because she loved Cowgirl Peg so much.
Later the kids got in line to pet Jazmine, who gave each of them
a "kiss" as they went out the door. Jazmine thought this was
one of the most fun days she had ever had. "Jaz, you were
really good on stage. All those kids really loved
you! Your life has a great message about
kindness and respect for others."
Cowgirl Peg said.

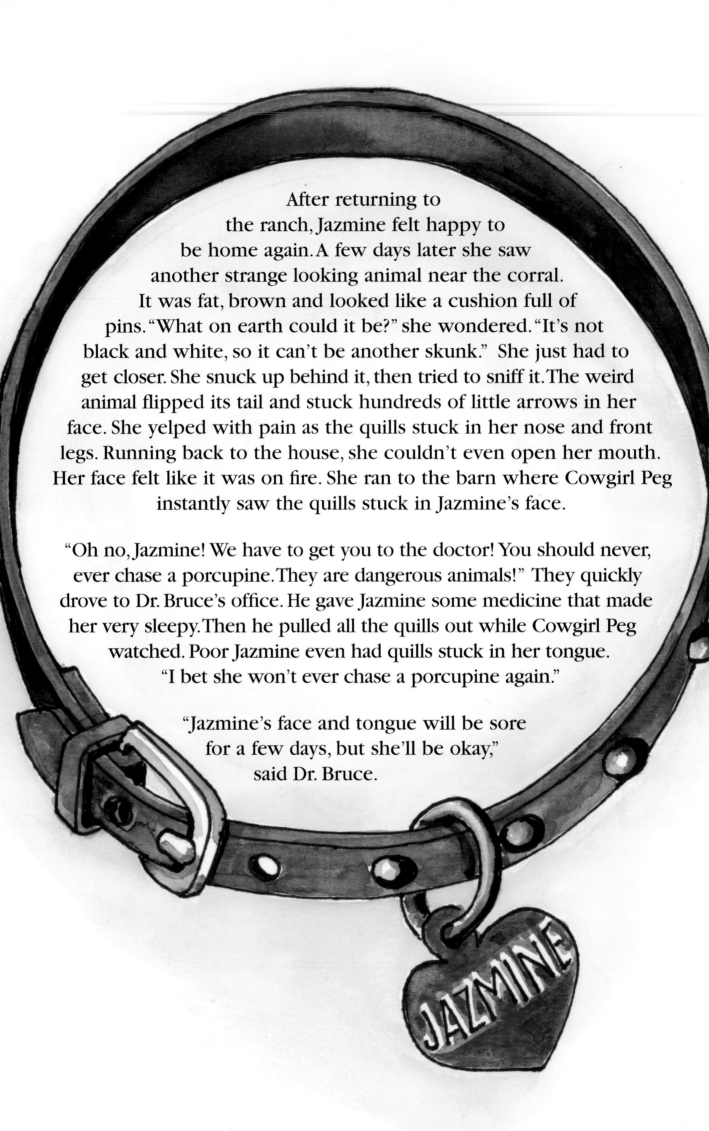

After returning to
the ranch, Jazmine felt happy to
be home again. A few days later she saw
another strange looking animal near the corral.
It was fat, brown and looked like a cushion full of
pins. "What on earth could it be?" she wondered. "It's not
black and white, so it can't be another skunk." She just had to
get closer. She snuck up behind it, then tried to sniff it. The weird
animal flipped its tail and stuck hundreds of little arrows in her
face. She yelped with pain as the quills stuck in her nose and front
legs. Running back to the house, she couldn't even open her mouth.
Her face felt like it was on fire. She ran to the barn where Cowgirl Peg
instantly saw the quills stuck in Jazmine's face.

"Oh no, Jazmine! We have to get you to the doctor! You should never,
ever chase a porcupine. They are dangerous animals!" They quickly
drove to Dr. Bruce's office. He gave Jazmine some medicine that made
her very sleepy. Then he pulled all the quills out while Cowgirl Peg
watched. Poor Jazmine even had quills stuck in her tongue.
"I bet she won't ever chase a porcupine again."

"Jazmine's face and tongue will be sore
for a few days, but she'll be okay,"
said Dr. Bruce.

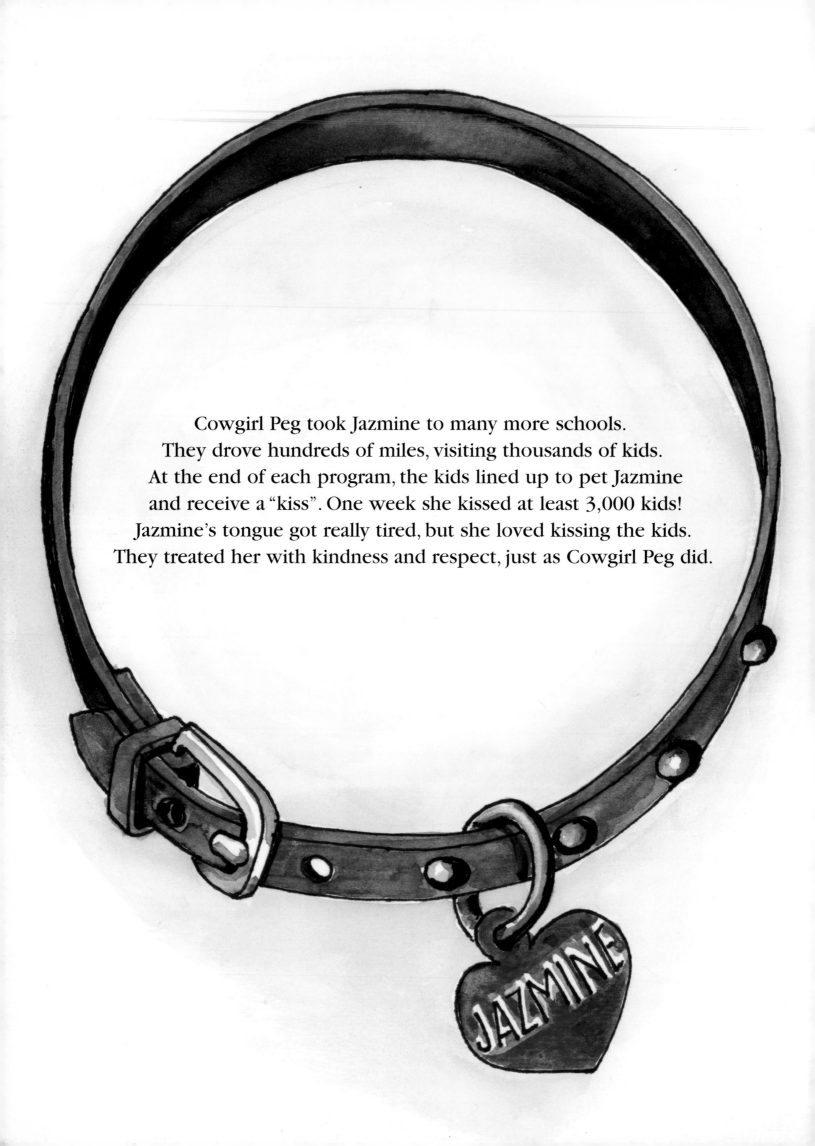

Cowgirl Peg took Jazmine to many more schools.
They drove hundreds of miles, visiting thousands of kids.
At the end of each program, the kids lined up to pet Jazmine
and receive a "kiss". One week she kissed at least 3,000 kids!
Jazmine's tongue got really tired, but she loved kissing the kids.
They treated her with kindness and respect, just as Cowgirl Peg did.

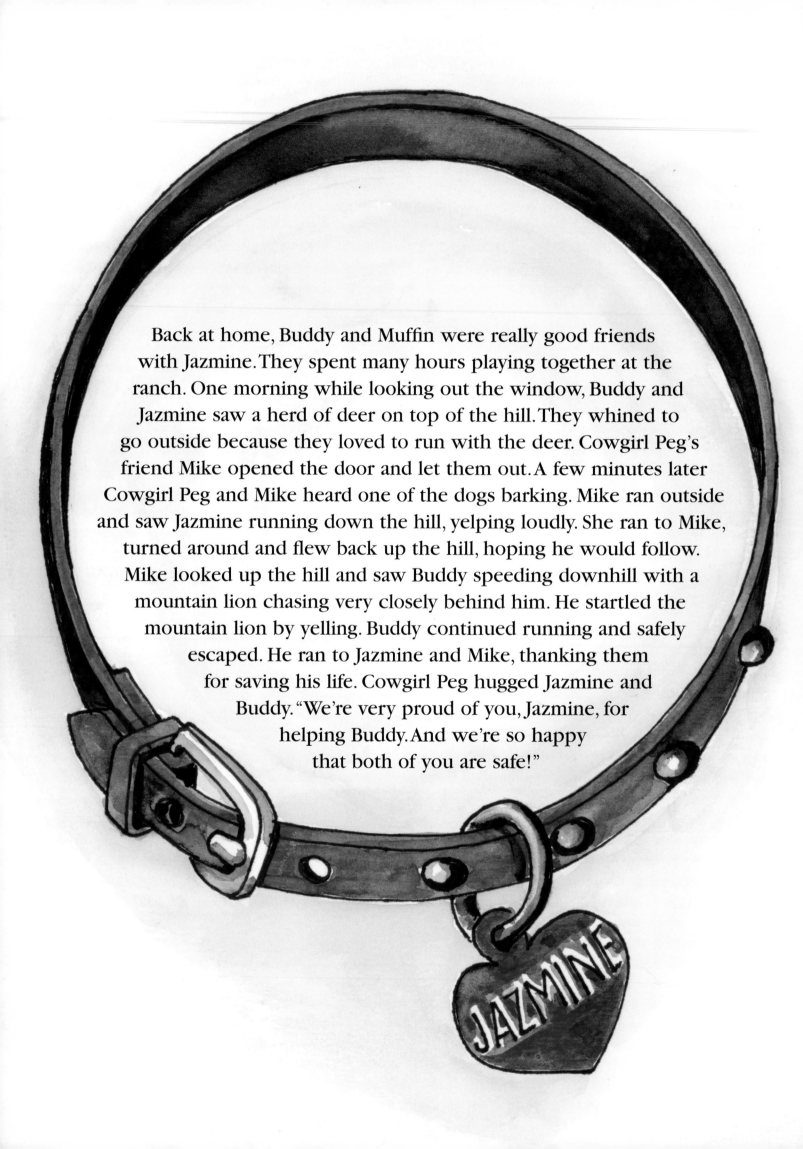

Back at home, Buddy and Muffin were really good friends
with Jazmine. They spent many hours playing together at the
ranch. One morning while looking out the window, Buddy and
Jazmine saw a herd of deer on top of the hill. They whined to
go outside because they loved to run with the deer. Cowgirl Peg's
friend Mike opened the door and let them out. A few minutes later
Cowgirl Peg and Mike heard one of the dogs barking. Mike ran outside
and saw Jazmine running down the hill, yelping loudly. She ran to Mike,
turned around and flew back up the hill, hoping he would follow.
Mike looked up the hill and saw Buddy speeding downhill with a
mountain lion chasing very closely behind him. He startled the
mountain lion by yelling. Buddy continued running and safely
escaped. He ran to Jazmine and Mike, thanking them
for saving his life. Cowgirl Peg hugged Jazmine and
Buddy. "We're very proud of you, Jazmine, for
helping Buddy. And we're so happy
that both of you are safe!"

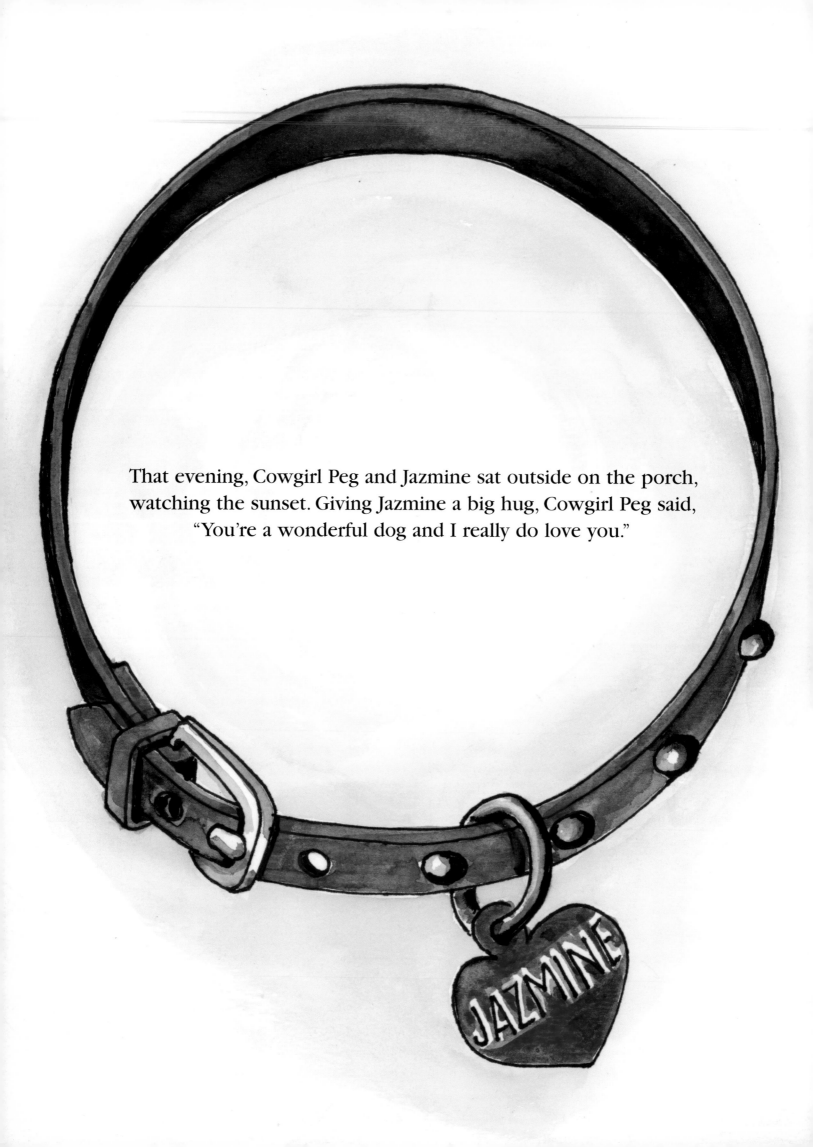

That evening, Cowgirl Peg and Jazmine sat outside on the porch, watching the sunset. Giving Jazmine a big hug, Cowgirl Peg said, "You're a wonderful dog and I really do love you."

Left and bottom center:
Jaz enjoying the attention of the wonderful kids at N. Davies Elementary School in Indiana.

Jazmine with her good friend Muffin

A Note from Jazmine
for the Kids and the Grownups

I want to thank the kind people at the animal shelter for providing me with a safe home when I needed it.

Now I would like to help other animals who need help like I did. A small percentage of the Jazmine book sales is donated to various animal shelters. Please support your local animal shelter!

From my heart, I say thank you!
Jazmine

Hiking in the mountains
with Cowgirl Peg and
Muffin

Cooling off in the creek

4-wheeling in the mountains

Playing cowgirl with the Santa
Fe Desperados of Kansas (west-
ern props provided by the
Kansas River Gang)

Having fun with Buddy
in a snowstorm

Cowgirl Peg and Jazmine

ABOUT THE AUTHOR

Peggy Sundberg Seeing her books evolve into a series that positively impacts the lives of kids is a dream come true for the author. Visiting thousands of kids nationally each year with Jazmine, she shares the books and their messages. Adding Jazmine to the program provides a touch of reality and leaves a lasting impression with students.

When at home, she enjoys the solitude of the mountains by hiking, biking or snowshoeing. She also loves spending time with the special members of her life — people and animals.

ABOUT THE ARTIST

Pat Wiles continues to awesomely illustrate the "Cowgirl Peg" books. *Jazmine's Incredible Story* is just another example of her artistic talents. The artwork in this book will amaze adults as well as children. Her wonderful illustrations greatly contribute to the success of these books. When not painting, Pat enjoys ranch life in the mountains with her family and a wide variety of animals, including her rescued wolves.